THIS

BOOK

BELONGS

TO _____

GROLIER
B O O K S

Disney's
SMALL WORLD LIBRARY

MICKEY and GOOFY DOWN UNDER
An Adventure in Australia

© The Walt Disney Company. All rights reserved.
Printed in the United States of America.
Developed by The Walt Disney Company in conjunction with Nancy Hall, Inc.
ISBN 0-7172-8212-0
Grolier Books is a division of Grolier Enterprises, Inc.

One day Mickey Mouse and Goofy went to the zoo to see the cuddly koalas from Australia.

"This is my favorite part of the zoo," Goofy said.

"Enjoy the koalas while you can," said Mr. Winsett, the zookeeper. "If we don't get more leaves for them to eat soon, we're going to have to send the koalas back to Australia."

"Gawrsh, there are lots of trees around here," said Goofy.

"These koalas will only eat a certain kind of eucalyptus leaf from Australia," explained the zookeeper.

"Why can't you get more of the kind of leaves they like?" asked Mickey.

Mr. Winsett sighed. "I don't understand it myself. We've been getting our leaves from the same company for years, and the deliveries have always been on time. Suddenly something's gone wrong, but I have no idea what the problem is."

Mickey glanced from the worried zookeeper to the children gathered around the koalas. "We can't disappoint the children," he said. "Goofy and I will go to Australia and find out what has happened."

"That would be wonderful!" said Mr. Winsett. "But it won't be easy. You see, I'm not even sure where in Australia the leaves grow. All I know is the name of the company that ships the leaves from Sydney."

"Who's Sydney?" Goofy asked.

"Sydney isn't a person, Goofy," answered Mickey. "It's a big city in Australia."

Mr. Winsett invited Mickey and Goofy to his office, where he explained that koalas eat only 24 types of the 603 kinds of eucalyptus leaves that grow in Australia.

"Unfortunately, the leaves our koalas eat are difficult to find," said Mr. Winsett. "Our supplier, Outback Imports, should be able to help you. I'll make arrangements to have a guide waiting for you when you arrive in Sydney."

After many hours in the air, Mickey and Goofy stepped off the plane in Sydney.

"I wonder where our guide is?" Mickey said.

"Maybe it's that guy over there," said Goofy, pointing to a young man who carried a sign that said, "Welcome, Mickey Mouse and Goofy."

Mickey stepped forward to shake hands with their guide, who introduced himself as Sam.

Sam had been told all about the eucalyptus problem. He agreed with Mickey that the first step was to visit Outback Imports and find out what the company knew about the leaves.

"The man who brings us those leaves is an old fellow named Dingo Dan," began Mr. Greene, the manager of the company. "We've been worried about Dan. He's never been late with a shipment before. But no one has heard from him in over a week."

"Do you think he's lost?" asked Goofy.

Mr. Greene shook his head. "Dingo Dan knows the bush like the back of his hand. I'm beginning to think that something has gone wrong."

"We'll do our best to find him," Mickey declared.

Mr. Greene pointed to a map of Australia. "Dan works around Alice Springs in the Northern Territory," he explained. "Start at the Jumpin' Joey Hotel. Dan checks in there when he's not out in the bush."

Mickey, Goofy, and Sam arrived at the Jumpin' Joey and were greeted by its owner, Matilda. She was also very worried about Dingo Dan.

"I think the special leaves Dan gathers grow along the Todd River," she said.

"No problem," said Goofy. "We'll just follow the river until we find Dingo Dan."

"It's not that easy," said Sam. "The Todd River runs underground, and the land around it is wild."

"Then we'd better get started right away," said Mickey in a determined voice.

Mickey and Sam loaded supplies into the car. They filled some cans with extra gasoline, and others with water to drink. They packed tents and mosquito nets for nights outside in the bush.

Meanwhile, Goofy had bought a boomerang at a nearby store. "Gawrsh!" he said as he practiced without much success. "If I learn how to throw this thing, I can play catch all by myself."

"Right now, you're playing fetch," said Mickey, laughing.

Soon the three travelers were bouncing over the dusty tracks toward the Todd River. Goofy came to a stop to watch a group of kangaroos cross the road.

"Kangaroos!" Mickey exclaimed.

"Gawrsh, why do the mother kangaroos carry their babies like that?" asked Goofy.

"Kangaroos and many other animals in Australia are marsupials," Sam explained. "Their babies are very small when they are born, so they are carried in their mothers' pouches until they are big enough to gather food on their own. Koalas are marsupials, too."

Suddenly Goofy swerved the car. "Yikes!" he cried, pointing to a strange-looking creature sitting on top of a big rock. "What's that?"

Goofy was so startled he forgot to watch where he was going. Crunch! The car banged into a piece of metal by the side of the road and groaned to a halt.

Mickey and Sam climbed out of the car.

"That's just a frilled lizard, Goofy," Sam explained. "In spite of the way it looks, it's harmless. It was just trying to scare us."

"Gawrsh," said Goofy. "It sure worked. And look at the car! Is there a repair shop around here?"

"About a hundred miles away," said Sam, laughing. "But don't worry about the car—I can fix just about anything."

Meanwhile, Mickey was examining the piece of metal that the car had hit. "What could this be?" he wondered. "This sure is a strange place to find a piece of metal."

Then Mickey looked up as he heard Sam's voice. "Hey, Mickey," called Sam. "Let's set up camp here for the night."

"Great idea," said Mickey as he trotted back to the car. "I'll gather some wood for a fire."

"I'll go down to the stream and catch some fish for dinner," added Goofy.

"And I should have the car fixed in no time at all," said Sam.

Mickey returned with the wood and began to set up
the tents. Sam finished fixing the car and pronounced it
as good as new.

"What's taking Goofy so long?" Mickey wondered. "I'm
hungry!"

"Me, too," agreed Sam. "Let's go down to the stream
and see if he's had any luck."

They grabbed two fishing poles and took off.

"Hi, Goofy," said Mickey. "We came to help you fish."

"Gawrsh," said Goofy. "I haven't even begun. I don't want to hit this funny-looking duck with the fishhook, but I can't get it to move."

Sam and Mickey laughed. "That's no duck, Goofy," said Sam. "That's a platypus."

"A what?" said Goofy in a puzzled voice.

"A platypus," Sam repeated. "Platypuses are mammals, but they lay eggs and have duck bills. We're probably near her nest. That's why she won't move."

Mickey, Sam, and Goofy moved downstream, and before long, they caught plenty of fish.

Back at camp, they watched the sun set. Sam pointed out Ayers Rock, a beautiful sandstone mountain in the distance.

Suddenly a loud howl startled the campers.

"Wh-what was that?" asked Goofy.

"Sounds like dingoes," said Sam. "They're wild dogs. Let me borrow your boomerang to scare them away, Goofy."

Sam threw the curved stick into the dusk. It whistled over the heads of the dingoes, then sailed right back into his hand.

The next morning everyone woke up bright and early. As Sam finished loading the car, he noticed Goofy playing with a little yellow dog.

"Goofy!" cried Sam. "Get away! That's a wild dingo!"

"Gawrsh," said Goofy. "I've never seen a wild dog with a collar before."

Sam and Mickey cautiously walked over to look at the
dog, who was indeed wearing a collar. The dog wagged its
tail happily.

"This one isn't wild," Sam observed.

"It belongs to Dingo Dan!" Mickey exclaimed, reading
the tag on the dog's collar.

At the sound of Dingo Dan's name, the dog jumped
up and began to run down the road. Mickey, Goofy, and
Sam followed.

They followed the dog to a clearing where an old man was sitting by a plane.

"You must be Dingo Dan," said Mickey, introducing himself, Goofy, and Sam.

"G'day, mate," said Dingo Dan, shaking Mickey's hand. "Am I glad to see you three!"

"What happened to your plane?" asked Sam.

"I can't figure it out," said Dan. "Something went wrong a couple of weeks ago. I made an emergency landing, and I've been stuck here with my dog, Digger, ever since."

"Let me take a look at your plane," said Sam. "Maybe I can fix it."

Sam walked around the plane. Then he said, "There's a piece missing here. We'll have to go to Sydney for a replacement."

"Oh, dear!" said Dan. "I promised the zoo a shipment of leaves over two weeks ago. How are they going to feed the koalas?"

Mickey thought for a minute. Then he snapped his
fingers. "I'll bet I can help!" he said. "Wait right here!"

In a little while, Mickey returned with the piece of
metal that the car had hit. "Is this the missing piece?"

"It sure is!" said Sam. "Allow me," he told Dingo Dan,
and he quickly made the repair.

"You're pretty good at fixing planes," Dan said to Sam. "What would you think about being my partner? This plane is almost as old as I am, and we both break down quite a bit."

Sam agreed happily, and he and Dingo Dan shook hands.

"Now the koalas are sure to get their leaves on time!" exclaimed Goofy.

Back at the zoo, the koalas munched happily on a fresh shipment of their favorite leaves.

"I'm sure Dingo Dan and Sam will be able to deliver all your shipments on time from now on," Mickey told Mr. Winsett.

"I can't thank you enough," said Mr. Winsett. "You and Goofy saved the day!"

"We're the ones who should be thanking you," said Mickey. "We had such a wonderful time in Australia. Didn't we, Goofy . . . Goofy?"

Mickey looked around to see Goofy lying on the ground in front of the koalas.

"Goofy, what are you doing down there?" Mickey asked.

"Guess what?" Goofy said happily. "I finally got the boomerang to come back!"

Did You Know...?

Every country has many different customs and places that make it special. Some of the things that make Australia special are mentioned below. Do you recognize any of them from the story?

Since Australia is located in the Southern Hemisphere, its seasons are the opposite of those in the United States. In Australia, winter lasts from June through August, and summer lasts from December through February.

Sydney, Australia's oldest and largest city, has sunshine almost every day of the year. Sydney is the chief port of Australia. Its spacious harbor is spanned by a bridge that is more than ½ mile long.

Australia has many interesting
animals that are not found
anywhere else in the world.
Kangaroos, for example, are found
only in Australia. They can hop as
fast as 40 miles per hour, and
jump as high as 6 feet.

The koala is named after an
aboriginal word meaning
"no drink." That's because koalas
rarely drink water. Instead, they get
moisture from eucalyptus leaves and
bark, the only types of foods they eat.

The Great Barrier Reef off Australia's northern coast
is the largest coral reef in the world. It is actually a chain
of over 2,500 tiny reefs and contains 300 kinds of
colorful coral.

The platypus, Australia's strangest animal, has a bill like a duck. It has a flat tail like a beaver, lays eggs like a bird, and lives part of the time underwater like a fish!

Boomerangs were first used by the aborigines as weapons for hunting and fighting. They are also used as toys, tools, and even musical instruments.

The aborigines were the first people in Australia. They have been there over 40,000 years. Many aborigines still live in Australia.

Ayers Rock is a large sandstone cliff about 1½ miles long and is a top tourist attraction. The walls of its caves are covered with ancient paintings made by the aborigines.

"Good on you, mate!" means "Thanks, friend!" to Australians.